Shiraz

Shiraz

By DC Fidler

DCFidler Publishing
2018

Published by DCFidler Publishing
1117 University Avenue, #505
Morgantown, WV 26505
DCFidlerpublishing@gmail.com

Printed in the United States of America
by Lulu Press, Inc.

This play is entirely a work of fiction.
Any resemblance to actual persons, living or dead,
is entirely coincidental.

ISBN: 978-0-9989729-9-2
Library of Congress Control Number: 2018909540

Characters

Lowell – man in mid 50s
Justin – man in early 20s
August – man in late 20s or early 30s
Charlotte – woman in 40s or 50s
Ludwig – man in 60s or 70s
Francine – woman in 50s

Setting

A simple kitchen during lightly warm weather in coastal North Carolina in late Spring 2004. There are three doors: one to outside, one to a back porch, and one to the other rooms of the house.

Appreciation

Thank you Esteban Ramos and family for years of friendship and for your kind hospitality in Santiago, Chile, sharing personal stories of troubling times. Thank you Andrew Lundquist for your friendship and sharing your enthusiastic, superb sommelier expertise.

Note

In contrast to formal scripts for use in rehearsals, this is a book of the script, containing more stage directions to aid readers to envision what can be happening upon the stage. Most actors prefer few or no directions, allowing them to discover and create the lives of their characters.

Shiraz premiered at the Monongalia Arts Center's M.T. Pockets Theatre in Morgantown, West Virginia on September 3, 2008.

Cast

Lowell	Donald Fidler
Justin	Shea Thompson
August	Jake Brady
Charlotte	Lydia Mong
Ludwig	Ron Weaver
Francine	Tammy Hoier

Staff

Director	Glynis Board
Producers	Toni Morris
	Vickie Trickett
Assistant Director	Nora Perone
Lighting Design	Glynis Board
Fight Choreographer	Kara Haas
Spanish Vocal Coach	Karina Thurston
Scenic Assistant	Ron Adamson

Act One

Red lights rise on a piano to one side of the stage and on a guitar on the opposite side.

LOWELL, dressed in pajamas and bathrobe, carrying an envelope and a bottle of wine, walks to piano and sits.

JUSTIN walks to guitar and sits.

LOWELL plays a brief Spanish tune on piano. As he finishes playing, JUSTIN overlaps the tune with his Spanish tune on guitar. JUSTIN finishes playing.

Red lights fade to black as bright morning lights rise on the kitchen center stage.

LOWELL, carrying the envelope and wine, walks to the kitchen where several opened bottles of wine are scattered about the room. He stares at the envelope momentarily, and then leans it against a small TV. He places the unopened bottle of wine on the table and reads the label to himself, launching him into a trance of remembering.

LOWELL is jarred into the present when there is a knock at the door.

LOWELL: *(Condescending, mocking southern accent always with this phrase, unhappy to be interrupted.)* Dee-oors opunnn. Keey'um on innnn.

1

(AUGUST enters.)

AUGUST: Lowell? The po-lease is lookin' fer me.

LOWELL: *(LOWELL'S regular accent.)* Are they? Which "po-lease" would that be?

AUGUST: Hogan and Murphy.

LOWELL: Cough it out. What happened?

AUGUST: I set fire to Tina Rae's porch couch.

LOWELL: And why, August Luther Perry, would one do that?

AUGUST: She said she loves Butcher now and ain't gonna go with me no more.

(LOWELL motions for AUGUST to sit.)

LOWELL: So, you took it out on her couch.

AUGUST: Where she and Butcher did it. Her "mauve" porch couch.

LOWELL: "Mauve?"

AUGUST: It's a color.

LOWELL: And all would be balanced in your world if her mauve couch burned.

AUGUST: They's sayin' it's arson.

(LOWELL hands coffee mug to AUGUST.)

LOWELL: "Arson" means deliberately setting a harmful fire.

AUGUST: And attempted murder.

LOWELL: Was she in her house?

AUGUST: It wouldn't upset her none if she weren't there to see it.

LOWELL: The house could have caught fire and killed her. Attempted murder.

AUGUST: It only made a hole in one cushion, size of a pool ball.

2

LOWELL: Thank goodness you lack arson skills.

AUGUST: I would never burn Tina Rae. Can I have half a cube'a sugar?

LOWELL: You have diabetes.

AUGUST: Jest a half.

LOWELL: Promise to call Hogan and explain?

AUGUST: I'm not calling Murphy.

LOWELL: Just Hogan.

AUGUST: Promise.

(LOWELL drops sugar cube into coffee.)

LOWELL: One half cube.

AUGUST: Are they gonna arrest me?

LOWELL: You'll be fine. Pamlico Sound justice.

AUGUST: They won't cuff and drag me off?

LOWELL: Hogan is your cousin. He looks after you. As long as an eager *Sun Journal* reporter doesn't blow it out of proportion.

AUGUST: Or CNN.

LOWELL: Or ... Hogan will assure the couch is repaired, assure Tina Rae is calm, and assure you are reprimanded.

AUGUST: That means scolded.

LOWELL: You remember. Good.

AUGUST: Kin I git molasses too?

LOWELL: Sugar is in molasses.

AUGUST: Not much as honey.

(AUGUST makes sad, puppy face.)

LOWELL: After you call Hogan.

AUGUST: I'll call him from Tina Rae's. She's bakin' me a strawberry pie fer scrubbin' the burn mark off her window screen.

LOWELL: Imagine that.

3

AUGUST: Bye, Lowell.

(AUGUST exits. LOWELL holds up AUGUST'S mug, knowing he will return. AUGUST returns and accepts mug.)

AUGUST: *(Exiting.)* This time, I'll bring yer mug back.

(LOWELL grabs a wrench, gets on knees, and looks under sink. He struggles to use wrench.)

LOWELL: Damn it!

(LOWELL stands, opens the unopened bottle of wine, smells the wine, and studies the label until there is a knock on the door.)

LOWELL: Dee-oors opunnn. Keey'um on innnn.

(JUSTIN enters, wearing preppy shirt, preppy sweater, baseball hat, and small backpack.)

JUSTIN: You sure it's okay if I come in?

(LOWELL places wine bottle on table.)

LOWELL: Oh. I thought you were my usual deluge of morning neighbors.
JUSTIN: Good morning. Nice to meet you. I'm Justin.
LOWELL: I'm Lowell.
JUSTIN: I saw you last winter at your sister's funeral. I didn't actually meet you. During her funeral I sat in Lena's car across the street.
LOWELL: During the funeral? That's quite strange.
JUSTIN: Your niece and I were friends in New York.

LOWELL: I didn't know she had friends. Always seemed standoffish.

JUSTIN: Not with me.

LOWELL: Let me get this straight. While Lena and the rest of our family attended her mother's funeral, you sat in a car across the street?

JUSTIN: Pretty much.

LOWELL: Was she embarrassed to introduce you?

JUSTIN: I wasn't family. Guess she was shy to ask.

LOWELL: More like paranoid. Must have adopted her mother's quirks. My sister Daniela was a recluse. Afraid to even socialize with birds around the feeder. Sneaked out at night to fill it.

JUSTIN: Uh, is it okay if I come all the way in?

LOWELL: Are you here to sell something?

JUSTIN: No sir.

LOWELL: Have a seat. But I won't buy anything, no matter how friendly you pretend to be. I have errands. Time for one cup of coffee. Then off with you.

JUSTIN: A glass of water will be fine.

LOWELL: I have bottled water. Tap water here tastes like swamp gas.

(JUSTIN examines wine bottle on table.)

JUSTIN: What kind of wine is this?

LOWELL: Leave that alone! It needs to breathe. I was working on my plumbing when you intruded. Drips. Rots the wood. I can't tighten the bolt under the sink.

JUSTIN: I'm pretty handy with that sort of thing.

LOWELL: There's the wrench on the floor.

(JUSTIN pulls off backpack and sweater. Wearing a sleeveless T-shirt, he stretches his muscles.)

JUSTIN: Here, can you hold my sweater?

5

LOWELL: Drape it on the chair.

(As LOWELL places a water bottle on the table, JUSTIN tosses his belongings on a chair, lies on his back on the floor, and uses the wrench to tighten a bolt.)

LOWELL: I tried like the dickens to turn that bolt.

JUSTIN: I've been working out steadily. I should be able to do it.

LOWELL: Working out in a gym?

JUSTIN: Four days a week.

LOWELL: One of those places with wall-to-wall mirrors, almost naked people staring at themselves?

JUSTIN: You know more about city life than I expected for a man living on the rural coast.

LOWELL: Sitcoms. Figure they have some strands of truth. *Friends*, *Frasier*. New drama, *Cold Case*. I like *Cold Case*. Do you watch it?

JUSTIN: Haven't seen that one.

LOWELL: Crime solving. Crimes from way back in time. People getting away with crimes for decades before they catch'em.

JUSTIN: Huh.

LOWELL: At my age, living alone, I stare at an abundance of unhealthy shows.

JUSTIN: *(Standing.)* There. That should hold it.

LOWELL: You have crud on your back where you mopped up my floor.

(JUSTIN brushes off his back in a showing-off-his-body manner.)

JUSTIN: Did I get it all?

LOWELL: Down lower.

JUSTIN: *(Brushing back.)* Thanks. So, you live here alone?

LOWELL: I try to. Neighbors drop by every few minutes, day in, day out.

JUSTIN: Lena said you used to travel, live in foreign countries.

LOWELL: Oriental, North Carolina is a foreign country. Are you spying on me? I don't fancy people prying into my affairs.

JUSTIN: I didn't mean it to feel like prying. My apologies.

LOWELL: Where's your family?

JUSTIN: Well, Dad died when I was little. Mom moved west to Aspen. I live in the New York area, work in advertising. Health food, travel.

LOWELL: How do you know Lena?

JUSTIN: We discovered we had much in common.

LOWELL: Meet at the gym?

JUSTIN: Actually, we met in the travel section of a New York bookstore.

LOWELL: City life.

JUSTIN: We reached for the same book on South America. Went out for coffee. Long story short, she tutored me in Spanish. The rest is history. Do you speak Spanish? ¿Habla español?

(LOWELL pauses to study JUSTIN.)

LOWELL: *(Condescending, mocking southern accent.)* Down here, I'm plum lucky to pronunciate English.
(Usual accent.)
What do you mean, "The rest is history?"

JUSTIN: Lena and I were … partners.

LOWELL: Business partners?

JUSTIN: Writing together. Living together. Kind of dating.

LOWELL: Good god. You dated my weird niece?

JUSTIN: Anything wrong with that?

LOWELL: No, no. Nothing wrong. Just that her mother told me Lena was a lesbian.

7

JUSTIN: Well, she sort of … went both ways. Fine with me.

LOWELL: I'll be darned.

JUSTIN: Does that shock you?

LOWELL: Is that your mission? Come down here, shock a country bumpkin?

JUSTIN: No sir, I was trying to … clarify.

LOWELL: How old are you?

JUSTIN: Twenty-eight.

(LOWELL gives JUSTIN a good look over.)

JUSTIN: Okay. Twenty-two.

LOWELL: And Lena?

JUSTIN: Thirty.

LOWELL: Cohabitation. Condoning unnatural sex acts. You two'll go to hell. Pope says so.

JUSTIN: Not for caring for someone. Maybe for evil thoughts, horrible urges boiling around in my head.

LOWELL: Well in that case, we're all in heaps of danger. Pope, too. Well, I need to head out for my weekly drive to New Bern. Grocery shop.

JUSTIN: Before you go, can I bother you for something else to drink?

LOWELL: You still have water. You're tricky like a salesman.

JUSTIN: Something other than water? Please?

LOWELL: Coffee? Tea? Tequila?

JUSTIN: A bit early for tequila.

LOWELL: Not the way this morning's going.

JUSTIN: Tea would be great.

LOWELL: Tea. Tea. I can do tea. Lipton. No fancy homeopathic, or metro-sexual, or group-sex teas.

JUSTIN: Lipton will be fine.

LOWELL: So, you and Lena.

JUSTIN: She was amazing.

(LOWELL prepares tea.)

LOWELL: Was? Already broke up, did you? Not surprised.

JUSTIN: I'm sorry to be the one to tell you this, but Lena died. One month ago.

LOWELL: Good lord. I hadn't heard. She looked healthy at Daniela's funeral. Well, that's a crying shame. What a warm smile she had, even when she was shy, crying at Daniela's ... Tiny smile but heart-winning.

JUSTIN: That she did.

LOWELL: So, is that why you came all the way from New York? To tell me this?

JUSTIN: I didn't think a letter or a phone call would—

LOWELL: No, no, in person is very considerate. But still ... My my.

JUSTIN: I'm sorry that a stranger had to tell you.

LOWELL: Daniela, now Lena. Land's sake.

JUSTIN: She admired you.

LOWELL: What?

JUSTIN: Lena admired you.

LOWELL: We hardly knew one another.

JUSTIN: She bragged about you.

LOWELL: I only ever saw her a handful of times. As a little girl. At the funeral. I do remember her big brown eyes, the way she put her finger on her chin reminded me of ... I should run my errands.

JUSTIN: No, please. Whom did Lena remind you of?

LOWELL: My mother. When Mom stood with her finger on her chin like that. Formidable.

JUSTIN: Lena stood like that when she was pissed at me.

LOWELL: *(Serving.)* Here's your tea. Had she been sick?

JUSTIN: She drowned. Middle of the Caribbean.

LOWELL: Oh my.

JUSTIN: She jumped from a cruise ship.

LOWELL: Oh my god.

(Taken aback for a moment.)

Anything else I should brace myself for before you harpoon me?

JUSTIN: Sorry ... She was wonderful. Creative. Left behind amazing poems.

LOWELL: I didn't realize she had talent to be a poet.

JUSTIN: I've lost several people close to me. No one like her.

LOWELL: I've been rude to you. I apologize. You caught me off guard ... You said your father died when you were young.

JUSTIN: Now Lena. And two years ago, a friend died camping in a snowstorm. Lost on Mount Washington. White Mountains in New Hampshire.

LOWELL: A snow storm?

JUSTIN: Two-day blizzard.

LOWELL: Did you find him?

JUSTIN: The rescuers used dogs, uncovered his body three days later.

LOWELL: Snowstorm. Hm. I wrote a story years back. Friends went camping in the winter, in the snow. During the night, one friend wandered onto a glacier. They never found his body. Out there, somewhere, the deceased friend lay ... Frozen, preserved in youth, whilst his friends lived, aged, withered away.

JUSTIN: We share similar losses.

LOWELL: My tragedy was fictional.

JUSTIN: Oh! Right.

LOWELL: You sure you don't want something stronger than tea? Wine? Tequila?

JUSTIN: I'm fine, thank you.

LOWELL: Well, I need something stronger.

(While talking, LOWELL examines wine bottlers sitting around the room until he finds wine in one. He pours it into his coffee cup and drinks.)

LOWELL: How on earth did you find me? Even if you did come down to North Carolina with Lena, Oriental is difficult to find. Even more for the "suburbs" of Oriental.

JUSTIN: I flew to New Bern and rented a car.

LOWELL: Flew to New Bern?

JUSTIN: I have my pilot's license, my own plane.

LOWELL: You're a pilot? Huh.

JUSTIN: 1980 Piper Saratoga. Older than I am. Most fun thing I ever do. Take offs—I love take offs. That power when you pull back, push the earth behind. Slowly bank to one side, then the other. Freedom. Have you ever flown a plane?

LOWELL: I prefer my feet on the ground.

JUSTIN: You seem adventurous.

LOWELL: Because I grocery shop in New Bern?

JUSTIN: Gliding low over Pamlico Sound was stunning. The horizon and water blurred. The slightest difference in hues. I wish I could have shared that moment with Lena.

LOWELL: She did well finding you.

JUSTIN: Because I fly a plane?

LOWELL: Because you're sentimental, handsome, strong, determined—

JUSTIN: Determined?

LOWELL: A man on a mission. You hunted me down.

JUSTIN: I owed Lena to find you.

LOWELL: You'll still go to hell. I learned that from North Carolina Senator Jessie Helms' election speeches. And from Pat Roberts' televangelism and before that Jim and Tammy Baker right there on my antique black and white twelve-inch Motorola.

JUSTIN: That is a small TV. When I first met Lena, she quoted Jesse Helms' speeches for my amusement.

LOWELL: She knew Jesses' speeches?

JUSTIN: Her mother mailed them to her.

11

LOWELL: Wow! I am bewildered. I thought Daniela and Lena ceased communicating. Huh. Senator Helms thought all of us who were educated would go to hell. He suggested building a fence around the University of North Carolina at Chapel Hill, so North Carolina would have "a great zoo."

JUSTIN: I take it you did not donate to his campaign.

LOWELL: No dollars, no pesos—peseta, no handshakes for politicians. Politicians are corrupt. Inflict damage beyond repair.

JUSTIN: A frightening view.

LOWELL: Sugar for your tea?

JUSTIN: No, thank you. Did you ever live in Chile?

LOWELL: In my imagination I lived everywhere. Why do you ask about Chile? Did you live there?

JUSTIN: No.

LOWELL: Visit there?

JUSTIN: No.

LOWELL: Study about the place?

JUSTIN: Some.

LOWELL: Right. Travel books.

JUSTIN: And history books.

LOWELL: What do your history books instruct?

JUSTIN: Uh, that the United States backed dictators to keep Communism out of Chile. That Chile has fine horses, fine wine, lots of copper. Chile is economically improving.

LOWELL: You sound like an entry from Encyclopedia Britannica. Cream?

JUSTIN: No thank you. So you have been there? Chile?

LOWELL: Three thousand years ago. Before electricity. Before human speech. Well, before free speech. Where in New York did you say you are from?

JUSTIN: White Plains. Just above—

LOWELL: Just above New York City. As kids, Daniela and I used to catch the train, the Empire Service from Albany down to Penn Station, grab a Nathan's hot dog, then Grand Central and up to White Plains, taking the uh, the uh—

JUSTIN: The White Plains Train.

LOWELL: The White? ... No. The Harlem Line. To visit our aunt. If you lived there you should know it's the Harlem Line.

JUSTIN: Lena never mentioned relatives in White Plains.

LOWELL: My mother's sister and her German husband. Died off long ago. Daniela abandoned baby Lena, left her with our parents, moved down to Oriental, said being near fishing boats resonated with her young life. Later, I joined her.

JUSTIN: Daniela. Valparaiso, Chile. Albany. Then Oriental—Then you in Oriental. Where you wrote your prize-winning novel, *Sacred Domain.*

LOWELL: My god. There's no way you heard of *Sacred Domain.* And it never won a prize.

JUSTIN: Lena loved it.

LOWELL: I'm taken aback she heard of it. My only attempt at a novel. I can't even recall what it was about. Well, that camping-glacier story. I remember that.

JUSTIN: I'm a struggling novelist.

LOWELL: You're definitely on your way to hell.

JUSTIN: I have a sketch of my novel, an outline. Maybe you can give me pointers.

LOWELL: I haven't written anything since before I painted anything. And my oil-paint tubes rusted to dust.

JUSTIN: You could coach me on my plot.

LOWELL: *(Pause.)* You're a tad off the deep end, aren't you?

JUSTIN: I'm serious.

LOWELL: Lord have mercy. What's your novel about?

JUSTIN: Lena used to talk about your family. I feel like I know them.

LOWELL: You can't help intruding, can you?

JUSTIN: A lesbian young woman—bisexual. Her reclusive Chilean mother hiding out in rural, southern, coastal North Carolina. Maybe a little bit about me, the woman's male partner.

LOWELL: Your novel revolving around you.

JUSTIN: The male partner's father's death.

LOWELL: Your father? How did he die? In real life?

JUSTIN: *(Pause.)* Let's leave it at that. I'm not ready to talk about him.

LOWELL: Are you ready to write about him?

JUSTIN: If I talk about him, I may lose my drive to write about him.

LOWELL: Pull secrets from your heart.

JUSTIN: From my bone marrow.

LOWELL: From both.

(JUSTIN pulls a folded paper from pocket and writes.)

LOWELL: What are you jotting?

JUSTIN: Additions for my outline. Young woman. Recently deceased mother. Suicidal drowning. Enigmatic uncle.

LOWELL: You're invading "my bubble."

JUSTIN: Research.

LOWELL: Even I didn't write about me in my own novel. I have Daniela's quirks, public shyness. I elect to remain on the outside, in the dark.

JUSTIN: *(Talks as writes.)* "He preferred to live in the dark."

LOWELL: More tea before you head back to New Bern? To your plane and fly north.

JUSTIN: I am intruding.

LOWELL: Yes. You are.

JUSTIN: I apologize.

LOWELL: Apology declined. Honey, sugar for your tea? A cookie, a wafer? Something to gobble down quickly.

(As LOWELL prepares a snack, there is a knock.)

LOWELL: Dee-oors opunnn. Keey'um on innnn.

(AUGUST enters, carrying mug.)

AUGUST: I called Hogan. He ain't gonna throw me in the slammer. Least not yet. He needs Tina Mae to write an after-David.

LOWELL: Affidavit.

AUGUST: Swear I weren't tryin' to burn down her house or murder her. Can you sign this piece'a paper 'bout my character? Oh hi. Sorry. I'm August.

LOWELL: August, this is Justin. Justin ... August. Justin was my niece, Lena's partner—dating partner. He's writing a book about Daniela, Lena, and me. Without my permission.

AUGUST: Oh. Okay. Nice to make your acquaintance. Will you sign for my character, Lowell?

LOWELL: Set it on the table. I'll read it when I get back.

AUGUST: I gotta have it right away.

LOWELL: On the table. I'll read it and sign it.

AUGUST: You won't drink and forgit?

LOWELL: On the table.

AUGUST: I can't let Hogan lock me up none.

LOWELL: I have company, August. Justin's leaving in a matter of minutes.

AUGUST: Well, I'll go tell Tina Rae. Bye.

(AUGUST walks toward door but stops.)

AUGUST: Oh, here's your mug. I licked the sugar off'a the edges so it won't turn hard.

(AUGUST leaves mug on table and exits.)

JUSTIN: August tried to murder someone?

LOWELL: It's a primitive love ritual. A dance of sorts. Last Thursday, Tina Rae knocked August out cold with her portable microwave oven. A couple of days post headache, August used his disability check to buy Tina Rae a new microwave, lighter weight, soft plastic corners. Here's a piece of toast, molasses, and a spoon for spreading.

JUSTIN: I've never tasted molasses.

LOWELL: Taste everything once. When I lived in the outback—Australia, I tasted kangaroo, crocodile, emu.

JUSTIN: Lena boasted you lived many places. Australia?

LOWELL: A sure-fire frontier. Everyone running, scared from something. Changing their names, hiding. I wanted to stay there, but Daniela demanded I move near her.

JUSTIN: Brother and sister, Lowell and Daniela. Lena used to say that Pamlico Sound was a world all to its own.

LOWELL: No way she knew much about our eccentric world. She grew up in Albany with my parents. I only remember her visiting her mother once down here. Summer before college. Thirty-eight days. Daniela counted them.

JUSTIN: Lena said her mother was too depressing to visit.

LOWELL: A woman hiding in her kitchen, chain smoking, swallowing Valiums. Her kitchen with the big bay view. Always looking out to sea.

JUSTIN: Looking for what?

LOWELL: She used to read poems hour after hour. Pablo Neruda.

JUSTIN: Poet Laureate of Chile.

LOWELL: Nobel Prize. 1971. Romantic. Brutal. He used to write from his home, Isla Negra, overlooking the Pacific. Did you know that he designed his home to feel like the inside of a ship? Daniela had that same sad, romantic connection to the sea.

JUSTIN: Lena showed me old postcards of Valparaiso beaches.

LOWELL: Daniela couldn't afford land on any true coast—of any country. So here, Neuse River, Pamlico Sound. Not exactly Valparaiso, but she found it ... consoling.

JUSTIN: Did you like it here?

LOWELL: It was a good place to write. A good place to paint. A not-as-good but acceptable place to practice veterinary medicine. Living in my father's footsteps.

JUSTIN: Lena never told me you were a veterinarian.

LOWELL: She never told me she liked both women and men.

JUSTIN: But you knew she was into women.

LOWELL: My sister blurted it out one morning after her ten o'clock coffee and Valium.

JUSTIN: Did it upset her?

LOWELL: Maybe that's why she mailed Jesse Helms' speeches to Lena. Hint at the immorality of it all.

JUSTIN: Senator Helms' speeches were not hints.

LOWELL: No. Not subtle. On the other hand, Daniela blossomed with delight anytime Lena found someone with potential for intimacy. I guess that included you.

JUSTIN: She stuck to me like glue. A brown-eyed puppy begging. Composing sonnets.

LOWELL: Sonnets? Wow. Deep emotions. Or was it shallow, promiscuous lust, like Jessie Helms preached most youth—especially northern youth—specialize in?

JUSTIN: Meaningful.

LOWELL: Meaningful? So ... not exactly monogamous?

JUSTIN: There was one woman. Briefly.

LOWELL: That must haunt you. Knowing Lena jumped from a cruise ship.

JUSTIN: Uh, it uh ... Unrelated. That was unkind.

LOWELL: When we discuss people with whom we connect, conversations risk danger.

JUSTIN: You're researching me.

LOWELL: The book in my mind. I have an entire bookmobile of unwritten novels up here. Tragedies. Comedies. Epics. But these days, pages, entire volumes disappear. Erased with a glass of wine, erased by a bad night's sleep. Snap. Gone.

JUSTIN: I keep notes.

LOWELL: You only jotted one note during your drawn-out cup of tea.

JUSTIN: I'll jot more later, when I'm alone.

LOWELL: My shelves are heavy with I'm-gonna-write-it-down-later blank notebooks. Preempted by one more blues tune, one more sitcom, one more shot of tequila. By the way, I think you and I stirred up enough that we earned the privilege of dulling our emotions and profound discoveries with fine drink. May I pour you a goblet of wine?

JUSTIN: Maybe later.

LOWELL: There won't be a later. Well, I shall indulge in a goblet of wine. Shiraz. My favored vice.

JUSTIN: What about this bottle you were admiring when I came in?

LOWELL: A special bottle. Reserved for later. I'll open up a not-quite-as-good but fine-enough Argentinian Shiraz.

(LOWELL retrieves another bottle and uses a magnifying glass to read the label.)

LOWELL: "Santa Julia Reserva, Mendoza, 1999." Good enough. "Jammy, vibrant. Easy drinking, vibrant strawberry jam, sweet fruit." Let me know when you tire of tea and molasses.

(Knock at door.)

18

LOWELL: Dee·oors opunnn. Keey'um on innnn.

(CHARLOTTE enters.)

CHARLOTTE: Hi Lowell. I brung ya a batch'a tamaters. Not as sweet as ... Oh, excuse me. Didn't know company wuz here.
LOWELL: Charlotte, this is Justin. Justin this is Charlotte. Charlotte has the lushest garden on Pamlico Sound.
CHARLOTTE: Hush! You embarrass me. Lowell lies to make me feel good. Don't work.
LOWELL: Pull up a seat and let Justin judge one of your prize·winning beefsteak tomatoes.
CHARLOTTE: I'll slice a few. Last year's wuz sweeter.

(CHARLOTTE gives JUSTIN a strong look over.)

CHARLOTTE: Good lookin' boy. I'll make myself a tea.
LOWELL: My kitchen is your kitchen. Someday you must taste her blueberry breads. Oh my.
CHARLOTTE: Stop it. Git back to whatever you two wuz blabbin' about.
LOWELL: Let's see. We blabbed about kitchen plumbing, blabbed about naked people working out in gyms.
CHARLOTTE: Goodness sake.
JUSTIN: Then about Lena's mom hold up in her kitchen.
CHARLOTTE: It's a miracle Daniela didn't move her bed into that darn kitchen'a hers. Never answered her main door. Never answered her phone. You had to go 'round back and pound fer'a hour. Finally she'd whisper fer ya to come in. She liked my soups though. Pumpkin, cold cucumber, tamater'a course.
LOWELL: Charlotte force feeds the entire water front.
CHARLOTTE: Keep it up, Lowell, and I'll take my tamaters home.
LOWELL: Okay, okay, okay.

19

CHARLOTTE: Sad Daniela had ...
(Whispers word.)
"cancer" like that. Jest grew weaker'n weaker, poor soul. We buried her next to her house so she could continue lookin' out at that ole sound.
LOWELL: Justin said he attended Daniela's funeral.
CHARLOTTE: I don't recall yer face.
LOWELL: He hid out in Lena's car.
CHARLOTTE: Her car? We wuz all grievin' heavy that day. How long you knowed Lena?
JUSTIN: Six months.
CHARLOTTE: Lowell? Go git that jar'a marinated cucumbers outta my truck so's Justin kin taste'em.
LOWELL: Cucumbers dripping in vinegar? Right away.

(LOWELL hurries outside as CHARLOTTE examines various wine bottles.)

CHARLOTTE: Look at all'a them bottles. I'll toss the empties ... This one's almost empty. So's this one, and—
JUSTIN: Uh, that one's full. He's saving it. And this other one, he just opened.

(CHARLOTTE smells bottle and makes face.)

CHARLOTTE: Stinky.
JUSTIN: Argentina strawberry something. How well did you know Lena?
CHARLOTTE: I seen photographs of her. Never met'er, 'cept at her mama's funeral. Brief like. Daniela had an artist's large touch-up photo of Lena over her mantel from when she was seven. Said Lena was the spittin' image of her father—Lena's father, Daniela's man. Lost at sea. I do believe she thought one day he'd sail in off'a Pamlico Sound. Guess seawater all connects.
JUSTIN: So, did Daniela ever date anyone else?

CHARLOTTE: Good men tried. She was beautiful, proper, fine educated. She wouldn't give'em the time'a day. I believe her heart died somewheres in South America.

JUSTIN: Chile.

CHARLOTTE: No courtin' man stood a chance.

JUSTIN: How did she lose her man at sea?

CHARLOTTE: I asked once. She shook all over. Screamin' in Spanish and prayin'. Spooky. I never asked agin. Weren't gonna risk that scene.

(LOWELL yells from outside.)

LOWELL: Charlotte? You got those "tamaters" ready?

(LOWELL enters with jar of cucumbers.)

LOWELL: I smelled their zangy sweet acid from way out there.

CHARLOTTE: Hold your britches. I can't eat my own tamaters, Justin. Cause my mouth to ulcer. Everybody else seems to appreciate'em. Here ya go. How is Lena?

LOWELL: Justin delivered tragic news. Lena died.

CHARLOTTE: Oh, praise heaven. Such a young, lovely girl. God have mercy. Did she leave children?

JUSTIN: Uh … No.

CHARLOTTE: Mercy's sake. End of a family tree. Unless Lowell here populated the planet in secret.

LOWELL: World is fine without my family tree stamped on it.

CHARLOTTE: Justin? Open this jar fer me. Don't let Lowell have it. He'll spoon out the vinegar and suck it down.

LOWELL: I would never—

JUSTIN: Yes ma'am.

CHARLOTTE: Any time, anybody mentioned Lena's name wuz the only times I seen Daniela smile. My my,

Daniela loved that girl. But she ain't never visited her. Never wrote her neither.

LOWELL: *(Mumbling.)* Mailed hate speeches to her.

CHARLOTTE: Never visited or wrote nobody. But she loved Lena, I declare.

JUSTIN: How can that be love?

CHARLOTTE: Love freezes some people up. Locks them in a prison. I seen it many times. Daniela had it the worst.

LOWELL: Charlotte's our local psychoanalyst.

CHARLOTTE: You and yer fancy labels. Lowell's even got Greek names fer my tamaters.

LOWELL: Latin names.

(He sings as if a Latin mass.)

"Lycoperiscon esculentum."

(Southern accent.)

"Tamaters."

CHARLOTTE: Either way, people eat'em. And big words don't grow'em.

JUSTIN: These are incredible. Not at all like grocery-store tomatoes.

LOWELL: Wickedly juicy. Intensely acidic. Red rich as steak tartar.

CHARLOTTE: After that, I'm leavin'. Anyways, promised Harland I'd help him clean his gutters.

LOWELL: Don't fall off a ladder.

CHARLOTTE: Hush yer fussin'. Even my mother still cleans gutters. My grandmamaw did 'til rheumatism won over last spring.

LOWELL: Dear god.

CHARLOTTE: Very nice to meet you, Justin. Keep your seat. See ya later, Lowell. Easy on that wine, ole fella.

(Whispers.)

Guard the vinegar, Justin.

LOWELL: Thank you graciously, Charlotte. Tell Harland hello for me.

CHARLOTTE: I will. Oh, Harland said the boat will be ready fer ya at three-thirty.

(LOWELL suddenly goes into a trance-like stare.)

(CHARLOTTE walks toward front door and stops.)

CHARLOTTE: Oh, by the way. Can you check out Toby? His hind legs seem to be gittin' stiff agin. Maybe another one'a'em steroid shots ... Lowell?

LOWELL: *(Pulled out of trance.)* Oh ... yeah. I'll swing by this afternoon.

CHARLOTTE: Don't wanna put down my ole horse yet, Justin. No good fer nothin' 'cept pettin', but he's been with me an eternity.
(She exits.)

JUSTIN: Your kitchen is a crossroads.

LOWELL: A watering hole. A parenting center. A place for legal counsel. A senior citizen center. Mostly a place for gossip. You can bet there'll be plenty'a gossip about your being here.

JUSTIN: Like what?

LOWELL: "Handsome young Yankee stud visits old dude." Anything you don't want printed in the tabloids. Spreads over the Neuse River and Pamlico Sound banks. Hope you weren't planning a clandestine visit.

JUSTIN: Well ... Not public.

LOWELL: Too late. Want some vinegar-weighted cucumber slices to chase those tomatoes?

JUSTIN: Uh, no thank you.

LOWELL: Well, I'll have a few. Mighty tasty vinegar. If you change your mind grab some. So where were we with your plot? Ah, yes. I believe you had a love interest in addition to Lena.

JUSTIN: That's not part of my novel.

23

LOWELL: Should be, my boy. Should be. Suicide is a multi-factorial event.

JUSTIN: Lena was obsessed over her mother's absence when she was growing up. She told me that the little bit her mother was present, she was like an, "emotional black hole." That was a quote.

LOWELL: Sounded like a quote. And you posit that is why Lena killed herself?

JUSTIN: That is why Lena killed herself.

LOWELL: Fine. But complicate your plot a tad. Foreshadow a bit of a lover's not being faithful.

JUSTIN: Not sure that fits.

LOWELL: Add other complications.

JUSTIN: Such as never getting to know her father?

LOWELL: Uh, you could.

JUSTIN: Lena said her father died in Chile, before she was born.

LOWELL: Disappeared in Chile.

JUSTIN: I read that under the dictatorship of Pinochet and his generals, thousands of young Chilean men who "disappeared," were never found. "Detenido Desaparecido." That's what they call them in Chile.

LOWELL: So in your novel, Lena's father disappears, "dies," which drives Lena's mother to prolonged grief, ultimately driving Lena to suicide.

JUSTIN: Something like that.

LOWELL: Throw in a few Southern senatorial speeches forwarded on by a mother distressing her daughter as foreshadowing.

JUSTIN: Her mother's letters weren't intended to distress her.

LOWELL: Your novel. Tell it anyway you wish.

JUSTIN: I'm pretty far along with it.

LOWELL: Then I'm sure the rest will write itself effortlessly.

JUSTIN: I need help on a few details.

LOWELL: You reject my suggestions.

JUSTIN: Please.

LOWELL: Good gosh. Let me see your rough draft.

JUSTIN: It's in my briefcase.

LOWELL: Bring it in.

JUSTIN: In my plane.

LOWELL: Your plane.

JUSTIN: The young woman based on Lena, I'm calling her, "Sofia."

LOWELL: As Chilean as "Lena" I suppose.

JUSTIN: Sofia's mother and her mother's parents move from New York to Chile.

LOWELL: Let me guess. The patriarch of the family is a veterinarian, a large-animal veterinarian.

JUSTIN: Tends to horses.

LOWELL: Details about Chilean horses?

JUSTIN: That they're famous.

LOWELL: Paint with words. Write this down, "Chile has the oldest breed of horses in the Western Hemisphere." Write that.

(JUSTIN writes.)

LOWELL "Begun in 1544 by a clergyman, Rodrigo Gonzalez de Marmolejo." Spelled M-A-R—

JUSTIN: I can spell that.

LOWELL: "Marmolejo's horses were used in Spain's fight against Chile's indigenous Mapuche People." Anchor your novel.

JUSTIN: One reason I'm here. To learn from a master.

LOWELL: I'll direct you to picture books about Chile.

JUSTIN: I can read, thank you. English and Spanish. Some Italian.

LOWELL: Excellente. Fantastico.

JUSTIN: I want to learn all I can about Lena's family in Chile.

25

LOWELL: Lena never lived in Chile.

JUSTIN: Her mother did. Her grandparents did.

LOWELL: Those people are dead. Respect them.

JUSTIN: How old was Lena's mother when she lived in Chile?

LOWELL: Don't show decency. Uh ... sixteen, I guess.

JUSTIN: When Daniela was sixteen, how old were you?

LOWELL: Uh, sixteen plus six ... twenty-two.

JUSTIN: You both were in Chile at the same time.

LOWELL: I suppose.

JUSTIN: So, the four of you, Daniela, your parents, and you. In Chile together.

(LOWELL walks to a window and looks out.)

LOWELL: This is my favorite time of year. Late spring. River and sound water still warm from yesterday's sun. See how the cool morning air draws light fog up from warm water? Treetops protrude from the fog, like in Japanese paintings.

JUSTIN: Nice.

LOWELL: Earth, sky, water ... boundaries blurred. I tried to capture that in my last painting. Twenty years ago? Twenty-five? At my age, time loses boundaries. Thirty years ago in Chile. Yesterday on Pamlico Sound. Blurred. I find beauty, comfort in blurred boundaries. I don't want a digital camera snapshot with brutally clear focus. Go home. Cry about Lena. Write your novel. Go to the gym and stare at your muscles. Have lots of sex.

JUSTIN: I need to find peace. Make sense of Lena jumping from the ship.

LOWELL: So, it's not about the book. It's about making peace with your tragedy. Justin? Listen carefully. Hundreds of generations lived and died, buried in tragedies. They did so without making sense, without

26

finding peace. But they moved on. I have groceries to buy, an ancient pet horse to examine.

JUSTIN: Please.

LOWELL: Move on, son. My advice. From my heart.

JUSTIN: Grocery shopping, horse examining. I could tag along.

LOWELL: Good god in heaven. Did Lena love you or did you chain her to a chair, force her to listen to you? You're like an Australian outback fly that persists in landing on your face, sucking that one last drop of liquid from your eye. No matter how much you swat, it never stops.

(LOWELL partially changes into street clothes.)

(JUSTIN gives a persistent, sad look.)

LOWELL: Sad "puppy eyes" don't persuade me.
(Looking away and back at JUSTIN several times.)
No ... No.

(JUSTIN gathers belongings and walks toward door.)

LOWELL: One drink! ... And then I'll teach you how to examine a horse. Not a noble Chilean horse, but an old pet horse with rheumatism.

JUSTIN: Thank you. Deeply.

(JUSTIN unpacks belongings and sits.)

LOWELL: I shall regret this. So ... Shiraz?

JUSTIN: Shiraz.

LOWELL: *(Pouring wine.)* Shiraz.

JUSTIN: So, you were twenty-two when you returned to Chile.

LOWELL: Already I am regretting our arrangement. 1973. Thirty-one years ago.

JUSTIN: To travel with your parents?

LOWELL: I had just graduated from college. Trip of a lifetime. Chile. The source for my parents' stories.

JUSTIN: Daniela was seventeen.

LOWELL: Sixteen.

JUSTIN: Six years younger than you.

LOWELL: I was required to shepherd little naïve Daniela through the maze of cultural differences, through the maze of sixteen-year-old pubescent tangles.

JUSTIN: But she became pregnant.

LOWELL: You did do your research. By one of the huasos— Chilean cowboys.

JUSTIN: I read about the huasos.

LOWELL: I am impressed.

JUSTIN: Pretty good horsemen.

LOWELL: "Pretty good?!" Best in the world. Elegant. Graceful. High cheekbones. Muscular. Not grotesquely but European-model like.

JUSTIN: You were attracted to this huaso.

LOWELL: I don't work out in gyms and lust after myself and others in mirrors.

JUSTIN: I didn't mean it like that.

LOWELL: Yes, you did. But I tell you, every human being was attracted to this huaso. Grandmothers. Grade-school teachers. His mother. He had a royal presence.

JUSTIN: No wonder Lena could seduce anyone she desired. Her mother was strikingly beautiful and her father was "European-model like."

LOWELL: Calm your hormones. Yes, this huaso had good genetics. The best. In fact, that is the beginning for your book. Describe the genetic traits of your characters. Tempt your readers.

JUSTIN: This is good wine. Fruity.

LOWELL: Carlos. Juan Carlos. Twenty-years old.

JUSTIN: In my book, I'm calling the huaso, Hermandez.

LOWELL: Never! Juan Carlos. There are names that command. Others do not. Juan Carlos.

JUSTIN: "Juan Carlos" it is.

LOWELL: This slightly stale bread goes well with that particular "not fruity" Shiraz. Cucumbers?

JUSTIN: No thank you.

LOWELL: Juan Carlos used to take me ... What name are you using for me in your novel?

JUSTIN: Thomas.

LOWELL: Thomas? My god. Do I look like a Thomas? I mean if you subtract thirty years and use your imagination.

JUSTIN: "Thomas" seems as un-Chilean as "Lowell."

LOWELL: A complicated story. Some other time.

JUSTIN: I have time.

LOWELL: I don't. What about "Tomas?" No. Rodrigo. At least "Rodrigo."

JUSTIN: If it makes you happy.

LOWELL: Not happy, but an improvement. So, "Rodrigo" and Juan Carlos used to ride their horses up into the mountains. Camp out.

JUSTIN: So, did you two often ride up into the mountains?

LOWELL: Twice. Camped, sipped on Mote. You know "mote?" Mote con huesillos?

JUSTIN: Hot tea, herbal, communal. You share one metal straw.

LOWELL: One straw. All day Juan Carlos asked question after question about ... about—

JUSTIN: About Rodrigo.

LOWELL: About my sister. What colors of flowers Daniela preferred. What songs stirred her heart. The second camp, Juan Carlos and I camped high in the Andes. He performed the cueca around the campfire.

JUSTIN: A dancing huaso.

LOWELL: It happened.

JUSTIN: I'm sure it did.

LOWELL: All huasos dance, smart guy. Cueca, usually a dance of a man in pursuit of a woman. But that night, a solo dance around our campfire.

JUSTIN: Striking image.

LOWELL: Sparks jutting up to kiss the stars.

JUSTIN: Romantic.

LOWELL: Two bottles of strong Pisco.

JUSTIN: No doubt.

LOWELL: He was drunk. Tried to climb onto his horse. Huaso's trust their horses to carry them home, automatic pilot.

JUSTIN: He left you on the mountain?

LOWELL: He passed out. Fell off his horse. I dragged him back to the fire. We bedded down by the embers, a light frost covering all grasses and rocks beyond that ... circle of warmth.

JUSTIN: Strong image.

(JUSTIN writes notes.)

LOWELL: Images. A matter of one's own perspective.

JUSTIN: Juan Carlos did not share your perspective of this "circle of warmth?"

LOWELL: Not his view.

JUSTIN: Did you ever ... you know, think of him ... you know?

LOWELL: Absolutely not. That was not a way of thinking back then.

JUSTIN: Some people did.

LOWELL: I was raised Catholic for Christ's sake.

JUSTIN: Oh, Catholic. Forgive me.

LOWELL: What is this? An inquisition?

JUSTIN: How did you learn Daniela was pregnant?

LOWELL: That's weeks, months later into the story.

JUSTIN: Pardon me for jumping ahead.

LOWELL: In the beginning, I was tricked, cajoled into letting my guard down about my single-minded baby sister.

JUSTIN: Juan Carlos tricked you? Ouch.

LOWELL: Ouch. Juan Carlos tricked his grandmother into extra empanadas. He tricked his grade-school teachers into ignoring his deplorable penmanship. It was nothing for him to dupe me into asking my parents for my baby sister to leave their shielded house and escort me to the Municiple Teatro in Viña del Mar. Later the Santiago Philharmonic Orchestra. BaFochi Folkloric Ballet.

JUSTIN: You felt used.

LOWELL: There aren't words.

JUSTIN: Jealous.

LOWELL: Used.

JUSTIN: By the Juan Carlos.

LOWELL: By a Juan Carlos. By Daniela. By fate.

JUSTIN: You demanded revenge.

LOWELL: In your fiction novel? If you choose.

JUSTIN: It follows. Revenge.

LOWELL: In shallow love? Sure. In true love? True love tempers deep wounds. You are young. You do not have experience.

JUSTIN: I am the age you were in Chile.

LOWELL: Then you are lacking.

JUSTIN: You get mean when you drink.

LOWELL: You admitted you were not faithful. You don't know what it is to be consumed. To melt yourself into another, not dependent upon the other even knowing.

JUSTIN: Juan Carlos did not know of your admiration?

LOWELL: He had melted into a different other, my sister. This is how the world moves. We romantics chase those who chase others. It keeps us electric.

JUSTIN: How do you know I did not melt into another?

31

LOWELL: You claim you are passionate about writing, but you left your rough draft in your plane. When you discuss Lena, your "meaningful" partner, you never use the "L" word.

JUSTIN: I don't like to use the "L" word.

LOWELL: Exactly. When you revealed that you were unfaithful to Lena, that there was someone else, it was with a shallow voice. As if someone at a concert asked how deep was your passion for the stirring symphonic music and you answered, "The popcorn was good." Even indifferent telling me my niece plunged from a ship to her death.

JUSTIN: Very, very mean. Not fair.

LOWELL: Never make your plot fair! People don't pay to read fair plots. Mirror the heart of the universe where existence is unfair.

(JUSTIN writes notes.)

LOWELL: Are you scribbling plot or my rambling?

JUSTIN: Both.

LOWELL: Good lord. Pour me another uh ...

JUSTIN: I'm not sure I should. You're becoming progressively spiteful.

(JUSTIN pours more wine for LOWELL.)

LOWELL: You woke demons long shoved under my carpet. Whatever damn thing coats this floor. Tequila. I need a shot of tequila. What about you? Oh come on. You are writing now. You won't lose it.

(LOWELL staggers to get bottle of tequila.)

LOWELL: Whoa. I am a bit off balance.

JUSTIN: I'll have a second glass of Shiraz. Only one more glass.

LOWELL: Tequila for me. "Only one more glass" for you.

JUSTIN: What did you do when Juan Carlos and Alaina, I mean Daniela—I'm calling the sister Alaina.

LOWELL: Damn spot better than "Thomas."

JUSTIN: I changed it to "Rodrigo." What did you do?

LOWELL: I went to the Philharmonic. To the Folklloric Ballet. To the Teatro.

JUSTIN: Alone?

LOWELL: What was I to do? Fetch a street urchin for company?

JUSTIN: Take a friend.

LOWELL: I didn't have friends in Chile. Family acquaintances would have snitched to our parents.

JUSTIN: So, you were alone.

LOWELL: Worse than alone. Imagine laboring to enjoy a symphony while in your head your heroic huaso is running his fingers over your baby sister's bare flesh.

JUSTIN: I'd vomit.

LOWELL: But there you sit. A French Renaissance opera chair surrounded by grandmotherly matrons of the arts. Black lace, cameo pendants. Fanning themselves. Seconds crawl by at execootion speed.

JUSTIN: Execootion?

LOWELL: Slow ... ly.

JUSTIN: Got it.

LOWELL: *(Mocking southern accent.)* Time fer 'nother company.

JUSTIN: Pardon me?

LOWELL: I never reminisce this long without neighbors barging in.

JUSTIN: This talk is cathartic for you.

LOWELL: The truth, Justin? You make me lust ... for absolute amnesia. If you were not my new friend, pardon me, meaningful partner of my sister's deceased

33

daughter, suicided daughter, I'd far and feather you outta town.

JUSTIN: I want to learn about Lena's family.

LOWELL: I'm finished talking about Lena's family.

(LOWELL walks to envelope leaning on TV, takes out note, and silently reads it.)

JUSTIN: *(After lengthy pause.)* Please.

LOWELL: *(Preoccupied, monotone.)* Write about her family from your imagination. Make peace in your imagination.

JUSTIN: But I am learning truth from you.

LOWELL: *(Still monotone.)* People don't want truth. Truth destroys them. Why we numb ourselves from truth. Wine, sex, CNN.

(Knock at door.)

(LOWELL places note back in envelope as talks.)

LOWELL: Ah. Perfect timing. Dee·oors opunnn. Keey'um on innnn.

(They freeze in place as bright morning lights cross fade to red lights.)

Curtain

Act Two

Red lights rise on kitchen. LOWELL and JUSTIN are in the same positions prior to intermission. Red lights cross fade to bright morning lights.

Knock at door.

LOWELL: Dee-oors opunnn. Keey'um on innnn.

(LUDWIG enters.)

LUDWIG: Hi Lowell. Who's yer young friend?
LOWELL: Who said he was my friend? August or Charlotte?
LUDWIG: Both.
LOWELL: Warned you, Justin. Talk here travels through superconductors.
LUDWIG: Real polite, too.
JUSTIN: Thank you.
LUDWIG: August said so.
    (Checks out JUSTIN.)
    Yep. One fine-looking fella.
JUSTIN: Thank you.
LUDWIG: Charlotte said so. Lowell? You got any maters and cucumbers?
LOWELL: You just talked to Charlotte. You know I do. Pull up a seat.
LUDWIG: You gotta have cukes to chase maters.
JUSTIN: So, I learned.
LOWELL: Ludwig, this is Justin. Justin, this is—

(He sings first notes of Beethoven's Fifth Symphony.)

LOWELL: Ludwig.

LUDWIG: Mama liked that Beethoven fella's music. August said you and Daniela's girl wuz together. You know, a couple. Zat right?

JUSTIN: We were close.

LOWELL: A naked fella who goes to gyms.

JUSTIN: Uh ... Gym clothes.

LUDWIG: I ain't prejudicial. People have their own ways. Up the river a bit, used to be a farm. Lloyd and Henry owned it.

LOWELL: Oh god. Lloyd and Henry.

(LOWELL gathers large <u>New York Times</u> newspaper from shelf and walks to door.)

LOWELL: You boys excuse me while I ... powder my nose.

(LOWELL exits from kitchen into house.)

LUDWIG: What's he been drinkin'?

JUSTIN: Shiraz.

LUDWIG: Is sherry-oz a liquor or a varnish?

JUSTIN: A wine. And he had some tequila.

LUDWIG: He is partial to his tequila.

JUSTIN: You were telling me about Lloyd and—

LUDWIG: Lloyd and Henry. Lived on their farm 'round forty year. No one said a thing 'bout it. Only one bed. Big bed mind you. Big fellas. Three-eighty each. Henry died first. Lloyd's heart broke. Died two months later. God bless'em. Sorry to hear 'bout Lena.

JUSTIN: Thank you.

LUDWIG: Charlotte tode me. You holdin' up?

JUSTIN: I'm managing, thank you.

LUDWIG: Charlotte said you wuz strong. Writin' a book August tode her.

JUSTIN: Uh, trying to.

LUDWIG: 'Bout the doc and Daniela.

JUSTIN: Loosely.

LUDWIG: Doc's a great vet. Saved my sheep when they got bloated. But he caters to horses.

JUSTIN: I learned that today.

LUDWIG: One time, Jenny Barefoot, two mile up the sound, had a hard workin' plow horse. Smokey. Give to her by her grandpa. Well, when her grandpa passed on, ole Smokey seemed to carry on her grandpa's spirit, if you know what I mean. Then Smokey broke his leg. Doc's the best but nothin' to do but ease Smokey outta this world. 'Fore he did, Doc here talked Reverend Hodges, High Tide Funeral Home, into lettin' Smokey be buried right smack next to Jenny's grandpa. Granted rights of a human bein'. Huge comfort to Jenny. Kept her goin'.
(Yells.)
Say Lowell, you got pepper for these cukes?

LOWELL: *(Yells offstage.)* On the table.

LUDWIG: Well dang if I ain't goin' blind.

JUSTIN: Did Daniela ever talk about Chile?

LUDWIG: Chili peppers?

JUSTIN: The country Chile. When she lived there.

LUDWIG: Oh, I thought you meant—Not much. Weren't a big talker. Had photos'a Chile. A course I'm nosy. I asked time to time. Real purty country. Cowboys still ranch there you know. Snow high up. Winter's backwards. Comes in July. That must be weird fer'em. Once we wuz hold up together, Hurricane Hugo. No power. Had to stay in most'a two nights. Daniela said it reminded her'a curfews in Chile. Said by five pm every day, every single body had to stay indoor on account they'd git shot if they gone out. Mothers sneaked out in the night, riskin' their lives to git milk'n bread fer little children. Weren't many men left. Men disappeared. Government grabin'em, takin'em in the night.

JUSTIN: That's scary.

LUDWIG: I suspected, 'though Daniela never tode me, some man close to her was took. In her wallet, she had this raggedy photo of a cowboy fella. I seen it when she paid me to repair screens Hugo tore off. I said, "Miss Daniela, that looks like one'a them Chile cowboys." She said it was jest an old magazine ad she saved. Suppose it reminded her'a somebody.

JUSTIN: A huaso.

LUDWIG: A what so?

JUSTIN: A huaso. The name for cowboys in Chile.

LUDWIG: Seems like they'd jest call'em cowboys or cowpokes or cowhands.

JUSTIN: They could.

LUDWIG: I never tode no soul this, but when I found Daniela sittin' in her chair, lookin' out at Pamlico Sound, deceased, I stole that magazine ad outta her wallet. At the funeral home, I sneaked up to her casket, slipped the picture ad into her dress pocket … Never tode nobody 'cept you jest now.

JUSTIN: That was a kind thing, Ludwig.

LUDWIG: Well, I best be goin'.

LOWELL: *(Yells offstage.)* You finished with your Lloyd and Henry story?

LUDWIG: You kin come in now, Lowell. I'm plum give outta breath.

(LOWELL enters and places New York Times on shelf.)

LOWELL: Did you tell him about Gracie and Emma? Justin'd be shocked to know we have lady lovers out here.

LUDWIG: Emma was my cousin, Lowell. I beg you respect that.

LOWELL: Sorry, Ludwig. I forgot you were related. Emma was a fine neighbor.

LUDWIG: Second cousin once removed.

LOWELL: Whatever on earth that means—but don't explain it again. Take some of these tomatoes with you.

LUDWIG: Much obliged.

LOWELL: Here's a Tupperware container. And take "cukes." While I graced the porcelain throne and thumbed through last month's *New York Times*, what stories did you lay on Justin?

LUDWIG: Little'a this, little'a that.

LOWELL: Little'a that.

LUDWIG: Little 'bout Daniela.

LOWELL: He already learned too much about our family. This guy's a spy.

LUDWIG: He's a good listener.

LOWELL: Spies are good listeners. Now he wants to help me examine Charlotte's horse.

LUDWIG: Poor Toby. I tried to talk Charlotte into gittin' a big dog, help her let go'a Toby.
(Shakes head.)
Stubborn. Careful, Justin. Charlotte'll stuff you fulla clams, shrimp, oysters, flounder, bushels of slaw, hush puppies.

JUSTIN: Sounds tasty.

LUDWIG: Pounds and pounds'a tasty. Thanks agin, Lowell. Always hospitable. Watch'im Justin. You'll learn a thing or two.

JUSTIN: Ludwig? Thank you for sharing your memories.

LUDWIG: Hope we git rain soon. Dry spell's killin' my baby corn.

39

(LOWELL exits outside.)

JUSTIN: Big hearted guy.

LOWELL: Big hearts around here are common as tobacco plants. You didn't touch your "one last glass."

JUSTIN: You don't offer your neighbors drinks.

LOWELL: Baptists. At weddings they toast with lime sherbet floating in ginger ale. They forgive my one vice.

JUSTIN: One?

LOWELL: One public vice. What memories did you pry from Ludwig?

JUSTIN: Did you know Daniela carried a picture of a huaso in her wallet?

LOWELL: No. Huh.

JUSTIN: Why would she do that?

LOWELL: Who knows why women think what they think.

JUSTIN: So, the government took Juan Carlos away.

LOWELL: Ludwig said that?

JUSTIN: He said Daniela told him the government dragged men away in the night.

LOWELL: The generals denied all such stories. Thugs of the night, whoever they were, came and went despite curfews.

JUSTIN: With so much danger in Chile, why did you move there?

LOWELL: My parents were born there. I had dual citizenship, even though I spent my first twenty-two years in Albany. My Chilean grandfather was a loud, outspoken ranch owner, highly political. He demanded Dad return to Chile. Dreaming Dad would become a mighty, governmental, elite person. But Dad loved horses. Granddaddy, my "viejito," died shortly after we moved there. Dad and I moved to his house, more inland, Melipilla. Mom and Daniela remained in Valparaiso, by the sea.

JUSTIN: Did you have a ranch in Melipillia?

LOWELL: Mammoth roaming ranch. Dad and I worked side by side, caring for neighbors' horses. Years before I attended veterinary school.

JUSTIN: And Daniela became pregnant.

LOWELL: For three months, our parents didn't know. Mom and Daniela moved back to Albany. Where the ... hit the fan.

JUSTIN: Mierda.

LOWELL: ¡Puta! La cagó, wea. Chilean Spanish. Mom told her elite Albany friends, "Oh, it happened at an opera ball."

JUSTIN: In Valparaiso?!

LOWELL: Lying was not Mom's forte. She announced that the baby's father was a wealthy, aristocratic boy who planned to move to Albany, wed Daniela at the "wedding of the century." I doubt the women's bridge club bought that line.

JUSTIN: No big wedding.

LOWELL: Lena was born. Mom shipped Daniela to a girls' school. Raised baby Lena herself. Dad and I returned. I completed vet school—Too much talk. Let's go rub down Toby, shoot him up with ketamine and steroids. I'll grocery shop. You fly home.

(LOWELL finishes changing into street clothes.)

JUSTIN: You have been generous. May I inquire about one more topic before we shoot up Toby?

LOWELL: Make it brief.

JUSTIN: These are great cucumbers. They do indeed cool the tomato acid.

LOWELL: That's not brief.

JUSTIN: Your vijito—abuelo—was political, vocal. It follows that your father and you were a dynasty of formidable political challenge.

41

LOWELL: A hair-brained conjecture.

JUSTIN: You know what? I'm sorry. I shouldn't have come. This was a rude mistake on my part.

LOWELL: Understand. I hate politics. I avoid politics.

JUSTIN: How is it the authorities took Lena's father, a simple huaso, but did not take you and your father?

LOWELL: We tended the military leaders' horses. Cured their favorites. They loved us. If you want something more sensational? Imagine it.

JUSTIN: I'm missing something.

LOWELL: Ah, Justin, Justin, Justin.

JUSTIN: I posit this, you sacrificed Juan Carlos, gave him to the police in exchange for ... something.

LOWELL: Good god. My grandfather was dead. Chile was collapsing. We had a comfortable home we could return to in Albany.

JUSTIN: The grand US. Loved by your sister, loved by you. But your father loved Chile.

LOWELL: He loved seeing his family thriving.

JUSTIN: Imagine this for a moment.

LOWELL: Dios mio.

JUSTIN: Your family was in danger.

LOWELL: We were not.

JUSTIN: In exchange for giving "the thugs" information about Juan Carlos, your family was granted safety.

LOWELL: Our ranch was one big family, including our huasos.

JUSTIN: Juan Carlos confided in Daniela?

LOWELL: Their universes revolved around their hearts being one.

JUSTIN: He told Daniela about his hatred for the military generals.

LOWELL: Everyone hated the generals. Later, everyone hated Pinochet.

JUSTIN: Many people supported them.

LOWELL: I have no patience for arguing vulgarities of politics.

JUSTIN: Daniela told you of Juan Carlos' hatred.

LOWELL: She used to go on and on about this boy, this young foolish huaso.

JUSTIN: You loved him, too.

LOWELL: Everyone was infatuated by him. I told you!

JUSTIN: You had enough information to turn him in.

LOWELL: Why would I, of all people, turn him in?

JUSTIN: Your sister stole his love from you, carried his child. You handed Juan Carlos over.

LOWELL: To save my family, you imbecile! The generals were dragging families away. My parents did nothing but good every day. They were devoted to Daniela. To me. The generals ordered me to give them someone. There was only one person I could give them!
(Pause.)
Good god ... I have never told anyone that. Not even myself. I'm gonna be sick.

JUSTIN: Truth. Not that hard to speak.

(LOWELL vomits into trashcan.)

JUSTIN: Lena told me she thought that's what happened.

LOWELL: Lena didn't know.

JUSTIN: She patched pieces of stories together. She concluded that you turned her father in.

LOWELL: To save my family! Even God understands such desperation.

JUSTIN: God? You sent a man to his death because he rejected your love.

LOWELL: You know nothing! Protecting family above all else, even above the one time in life you felt love. I sacrificed four decades of my life to watch after my sister, while people like you work out in "the gym." Did your mother pay for your school, give you a plane? Do

43

you have a trust fund? Live off the interest? Travel to exotic places where common people like me never go. SCUBA dive, wind surf, helicopter ski.

JUSTIN: I snowboard.

LOWELL: Spoiled, shallow brat. I didn't see it before, but now I see.

JUSTIN: You didn't witness Lena with a broken heart. I did.

LOWELL: Broken heart? You want to hear about a broken heart? You said Daniela carried a magazine ad of a stranger, an unknown huaso. I carry a real photograph. Juan Carlos. I took it with these hands. When we camped.

(He pulls photo from his wallet and holds it for JUSTIN to view.)

LOWELL: See? Paper. Paper and ink. I tear it up for you.

(He rips photo, allowing pieces to fall to floor.)

LOWELL: There. This memory brings nothing good for me. It brings no one back to life. It erases no guilt. Make your peace. Write your novel. Sell a million copies. Let it sit on a shelf. My confession changes nothing.

(He kneels and cries over photo.)

JUSTIN: *(Quoting from memory.)* "And the old man obsessed about the youth of his friend's face, frozen in time. A face looking out from a glacial coffin, speaking in the old man's sleep."

LOWELL: *(Pause.)* You did read my book.

JUSTIN: I did my research.

LOWELL: You didn't have a friend die in New Hampshire snow. You made that up to win my sympathy.

44

JUSTIN: You're hiding other lies.

LOWELL: You fucking get out of my house!

JUSTIN: Shiraz.

LOWELL: What?

JUSTIN: I want a third glass of Shiraz. My last. I swear on
... Lena's grave.

LOWELL: How dare you lie you cared about my niece.

JUSTIN: I care. She made me cry, laugh. Her poetry. Her
whispers in my ear.

LOWELL: God curse you! And now what will you whisper to
her grave?

JUSTIN: That you confessed.

LOWELL: Fine! ... She should know ... One more glass. But
a new bottle. I earned it for ... for surviving you.

(LOWELL opens a new bottle.)

LOWELL: I have not raised my voice in anger for ...
decades. Then you desecrate my morning.

JUSTIN: I pressed you.

LOWELL: I pressed myself.
(Staring at floor.)
Oh.

JUSTIN: What's wrong?

LOWELL: My photograph.

*(LOWELL stoops, gathers pieces of photo, and places
them into his shirt pocket.)*

JUSTIN: Do you have a copy?

*(JUSTIN pours wine into glasses, dropping a tablet into
LOWELL'S glass.)*

LOWELL: You live with your computers. Scan. Copy. I have
my father's 1948 Olivetti Underwood typewriter. Old

like my little black and white Motorola. Twenty years ago, I bought a crate of typewriter ribbons before they became extinct.

JUSTIN: So, you are writing again.

(LOWELL stands.)

LOWELL: This story we talked about, just now. You upset me. So, now I must write.
(Squinting at bottle and holding at distance as reads.)
"Shiraz. Australia. D'Arenberg, The Dead Arm Shiraz, McLaren Vale 1998."
(Looking at back of bottle.)
I need my magnifying glass.

(JUSTIN snaps fingers for LOWELL to give him the bottle.)

JUSTIN: *(Reading from back of bottle.)* "Intense black and blueberry, creamy oak, jammy, richly fruited, linen-textured tannins, nice freshness."

LOWELL: Did you know, that the original grapes, the Shiraz grapes came from the village of Shiraz in Iran? Ancient capital of Persia.

JUSTIN: I thought that was a myth.

LOWELL: Muslims aren't allowed to make wine. In secret, some do. But Australia, Argentina, Chile? They grow Syrah grapes, call it, "Shiraz." It's not, but very fine. A toast.

JUSTIN: A wine called by another's name. A toast.

LOWELL: May my novel outsell your novel.

JUSTIN: And vice versa.

(They drink.)

JUSTIN: Hm. That is good.

LOWELL: Hm. Strange little, unusual taste. Bitter.

JUSTIN: Another toast. To the memories of people we loved and lost. To my father.

LOWELL: And to Juan Carlos.

(They toast and drink.)

LOWELL: Hmm.

JUSTIN: Hmm.

(They savor wine in silence.)

JUSTIN: Juan Carlos. Lost so you could save yourself.

LOWELL: Now why did you go and say that? We share a lovely wine. Savor it. No deep thoughts. Alone in this moment. This is enough. Young people can't sit still. Always looking before the moment, after the moment. We are here. Now.

JUSTIN: I appreciate your pained honesty. That was difficult for you to share. Kind. Now I want to do something for you in return. Something kind.

LOWELL: Then keep quiet and drink your Shiraz. For me, that would be a kind thing.

JUSTIN: No, really.

LOWELL: Yes. Really be quiet.

JUSTIN: You love Pamlico Sound?

LOWELL: I do.

JUSTIN: Huge sound.

LOWELL: From the middle, you cannot see land.

JUSTIN: So much to see.

LOWELL: Weeks and weeks of sailing and exploring.

JUSTIN: Let me show you Pamlico Sound from my plane.

LOWELL: Your plane?

JUSTIN: Fly over and around, take it all in at once. It's magnificence.

LOWELL: *(Pause.)* Come back some other time. I'll take you sailing. Water from a plane is not aesthetic like sailing. Gripping the lines, water and wind spitting in your face.

JUSTIN: I'll take you up on that. But today? My plane.

LOWELL: I don't want to fly in your plane.

JUSTIN: I am a superb pilot.

LOWELL: Before you occupied my kitchen and interrogated me, I did not know you.

JUSTIN: We share bonds. Love of writing. Love of art.

LOWELL: Bullshit.

(LOWELL stands, but is unsteady from being drugged.)

JUSTIN: We both have wrenching stories about loving people and losing them.

LOWELL: My head hurts.

JUSTIN: I insist. Fly with me.

LOWELL: Your flying trip isn't about me. It's about you.

JUSTIN: There is one more story Lena and I talked about. I want to tell it to you from my plane.

(Knock at door.)

JUSTIN: Shit.
(Imitates LOWELL.)
Dee·oors opunnn. Keey'um on innnn.

LOWELL: No more wine for you.

(FRANCINE enters.)

FRANCINE: Hi Doc. Oh. Company.

JUSTIN: I'm Justin. I was Daniela's daughter's partner, Lena's "meaningful partner." I'm writing a book about the doc here and his sister and how events in Chile led to countless family tragedies. I'm sure you heard about all that from August, from Charlotte, and uh ... uh ...

(LOWELL sings first notes from Beethoven's Fifth.)

JUSTIN: Ludwig.

LOWELL: Justin drank a bit much wine. Justin this is Francine.

FRANCINE: What the hell's he jabberin' about? I jest got off a my fishin' boat.

LOWELL: Justin? When people are fishing, they are outta the loop until the last fish is cleaned.

(While talking, FRANCINE looks through the trash and eats something from a canister in the trash as JUSTIN looks on with disbelief.)

FRANCINE: Nothin' bitin'. Third day in a row. So I quit. Midday or not. Planet's overheatin'. I swear.

LOWELL: Justin wants to take me sight-seeing in his private plane.

FRANCINE: Doc here's a good pilot.

LOWELL: No, Francine.

JUSTIN: He didn't share that with me.

FRANCINE: Flyin' since he wuz sixteen.

LOWELL: That's private and personal.

FRANCINE: I assumed you two are drinkin' buddies.

JUSTIN: We are. So, Lowell learned to fly *before* he moved to Chile.

LOWELL: I haven't stepped in a plane since I moved to Oriental. Boats are better. Tell him, Francine.

FRANCINE: Coast don't look good from the air. Gotta see it with a forty pounder yankin' yer line.

LOWELL: Offered to take him sailing.

FRANCINE: Say, you got turnips? Russell and the boys is comin' home from the cape and I can't find one darn turnip. Rabbits.

LOWELL: There's a basketful from Harland on the back porch. Help yourself.

FRANCINE: *(Pause.)* You ain't gonna fetch'em fer me? You that soused?

LOWELL: I don't trust leaving you alone with my nosy guest.

FRANCINE: Holy smokes. Strange even fer you, Lowell. Get'um myself.

(FRANCINE exits to porch.)

JUSTIN: So, you're a pilot?

LOWELL: Not superb.

JUSTIN: Francine said you were good.

LOWELL: In my local tall tales, I am an ace. In reality? Pathetic.

JUSTIN: Did you pilot in Chile?

LOWELL: Too many tricky currents with the Pacific slamming up against the Andes. Mom threw a conniption fit—as they say out here—when I informed her I wanted to fly. Would have been spectacular.

JUSTIN: Yes or no, did you fly in Chile?

LOWELL: A handful of times. Is that another piece for your puzzle?

JUSTIN: It is.

LOWELL: *(Yells.)* Francine? Did you find the turnips?

FRANCINE: *(Offstage.)* Yep. What's this blue contraption?

LOWELL: *(Yells.)* A power generator. For hurricane season.

FRANCINE: *(Offstage.)* Awfully puny.

LOWELL: *(To JUSTIN.)* When hurricane season hits, I fear you'll still be sitting here, irritating me.

(FRANCINE enters, carrying small basket of turnips.)

FRANCINE: Maybe I should git a generator. Supposed to be a rugged winter. One day, all'a this'll be under water. Ocean'll crawl right up to Raleigh.

LOWELL: I doubt that.

FRANCINE: Scientists said so. Tell'em, Jessie.

JUSTIN: Justin.

FRANCINE: Justin. Learnt it from the Discovery Channel.

LOWELL: Maybe you should buy coastal land outside of Raleigh.

FRANCINE: My farm'll be under water. Strawberries and mint by the tool shed my grandmother Hedley started. Corn my great, great grandfather McKay had began. I swear. You boys dry out. Hear?
(She exits.)

JUSTIN: People hang onto land a long time around here.

LOWELL: August, Charlotte, Ludwig, and now Francine all visited and left. You're still here.

JUSTIN: Together, we drink.

LOWELL: Bottoms up.

(LOWELL guzzles drink.)

LOWELL: Finished.

JUSTIN: This is a good Shiraz. I'll sip. Don't let me stop you from imbibing another.

LOWELL: I shall imbibe.

JUSTIN: What if ... What if giving information about a simple huaso was not enough?

LOWELL: You make my chest hurt. Bad enough we learned global warming is threatening everything this side of Raleigh.

JUSTIN: Turning over information about a simple huaso was enough to allow Daniela and your mother to leave Chile.

(LOWELL stands and looks toward bedroom door. Maybe he should get his gun.)

JUSTIN: But your father?

LOWELL: Three bottles of Dead Arm Shiraz in my wine cellar. Bedroom closet actually, but it maintains favorable temperature and humidity. I'll grab you a bottle. Take it with you.

(LOWELL walks toward bedroom.)

(JUSTIN blocks LOWELL.)

JUSTIN: Your father had a big price on his head. The generals demanded more.

LOWELL: Two huasos. Maybe they asked me to throw in two huasos. I'll give you three bottles to leave now.

JUSTIN: Not two huasos.

LOWELL: Four.

(LOWELL hands JUSTIN'S glass to him.)

LOWELL: Sip faster and go.

JUSTIN: A pilot.

LOWELL: A pilot? Okay. Four huasos, one pilot, two grocery clerks, and a baker. Drink your—No. Take your glass. A gift from me to you. Take the bottle. Here.

(LOWELL hands the bottle he has been allowing to air to JUSTIN.)

LOWELL: Sip all the way to New Bern. Sip flying north to your trust funds. I'll fetch the other bottles for you.

(JUSTIN grabs LOWELL.)

JUSTIN: The generals demanded for you to be a pilot.
LOWELL: Your imagination is far off.
JUSTIN: The generals terrorized and used suck-at-it, "pathetic" pilots like you to fly their helicopters.
LOWELL: I wasn't capable of flying helicopters.
JUSTIN: Sure you were.
LOWELL: You're a born writer headed for a children's book award.
JUSTIN: Fly out over the sea. Fly back. Out over the sea. Back.
LOWELL: Atlantic sightseeing tours.
JUSTIN: Pacific. At night.
LOWELL: Moonlight tours.
JUSTIN: No moonlight. Blackness.

(LOWELL staggers to chair and gets JUSTIN'S sweater and hat. In a drugged manner he tries to put them on JUSTIN.)

LOWELL: Here's your baseball cap, your sweater.
JUSTIN: Cargo.
LOWELL: Put your clothes on.
JUSTIN: Special cargo.
LOWELL: I feel light headed.
JUSTIN: I dropped a tablet into your wine.
LOWELL: You poisoned me?
JUSTIN: To relax you.
LOWELL: I gotta sit.

(JUSTIN backs LOWELL into a soft chair, and then hoovers over him from back of chair.)

LOWELL: I don't want to relax!
JUSTIN: I want you calm for our trip.
LOWELL: *(Yells.)* No trip!

(LOWELL tries to stand but JUSTIN pulls him back into the chair.)

JUSTIN: You will be my cargo.
LOWELL: No!
JUSTIN: We'll fly out over Pamlico Sound. I'll fly back.
LOWELL: No.
JUSTIN: No moon tonight.
LOWELL: No.
JUSTIN: Dark. My special cargo. Like the young men in Chile. A few were old, like you, but mostly young men.
LOWELL: Young.
JUSTIN: Sedated. Calm. No resistance.
LOWELL: I won't fly with you.
JUSTIN: Dozens of young men. Your cargo.
LOWELL: Young men.
JUSTIN: In the back of the helicopter when you flew over the Pacific.
LOWELL: I couldn't see them.
JUSTIN: Cargo lost at sea.
LOWELL: Lost.
JUSTIN: Dropped from your helicopter.
LOWELL: I didn't know.
JUSTIN: You were only the simple pilot.
LOWELL: Once ... in the metal, in the shiny metal on the instrument panel, I saw a young man in back, on the floor. His eyes stared into my eyes.
JUSTIN: Juan Carlos maybe.

LOWELL: Looked like him.

JUSTIN: Daniela's boyfriend. Lena's father.

LOWELL: My co-pilot, an old soldier, Fernando, smelling like cigars and piss, climbed into the back. I flew in the dark. Five, ten minutes, not looking. I heard doors open. Wind. Then quiet. The helicopter flew lighter. Fernando returned, vomited. He whispered, "Vamos a casa."

JUSTIN: "Let's go home." Well, I've had enough wine.

LOWELL: Every night, my dreams. Brown eyes in the shiny metal.

JUSTIN: I'll help you to my car.

(JUSTIN tries to pull LOWELL out of the chair. LOWELL resists, pushes JUSTIN away.)

LOWELL: Juan Carlos. Maybe he was in another helicopter— Maybe no helicopter—Maybe he's alive.

JUSTIN: He's not. He drowned.

(LOWELL slowly staggers, looks out window.)

LOWELL: I look over the sound. Dream I am over water, air on my face, rushing up from the black. Faster. Pulling me home to the ocean.

JUSTIN: Lena said you were crazy.

LOWELL: The young man's eyes in back ask for me. Juan Carlos asks for me. I prayed for this journey. You can help me.

(LOWELL turns to JUSTIN, points at the envelope by the TV, and sits with his back to JUSTIN.)

(JUSTIN pulls out a note and reads it.)

JUSTIN: You're fucking suicidal?! No! You are *not* going out that way!

LOWELL: Harlan has a boat waiting for me.
JUSTIN: You are *not* going in a boat!

(JUSTIN rushes to LOWELL.)

JUSTIN: Lowell? Look at me!

(JUSTIN turns chair with LOWELL in it toward him.)

JUSTIN: *(Yells.)* Look at me!

(JUSTIN kneels on floor, forcing LOWELL to look into his eyes.)

LOWELL: I am looking.

(LOWELL turns away and JUSTIN forces LOWELL'S head back to looking at him.)

JUSTIN: You know why Lena and I were drawn to each other? Why we instantly sensed a deep bond?
LOWELL: Poems?

(JUSTIN slaps LOWELL.)

JUSTIN: She doesn't write poems. We were drawn to each other because we, Lena and I, both lost our fathers in Chile.
LOWELL: Your father disappeared?
JUSTIN: Died! Pilots like you murdered our fathers, you fucking son of a bitch. And now you're going to die the same way.

(JUSTIN grabs LOWELL and drags him across the floor.)

LOWELL: Don't hurt me! Don't hurt me!

(JUSTIN kicks LOWELL in the ribs.)

JUSTIN: Our fathers were alive when you fucking monsters threw them out.

(LOWELL rolls onto his back. JUSTIN straddles LOWELL on the floor.)

LOWELL: Stop it! I'll go with you! Okay? Calm. Be calm.
JUSTIN: Son of a bitch.

(JUSTIN slaps LOWELL.)

LOWELL: I'm sorry. I'm sorry.
JUSTIN: You're not sorry.

(JUSTIN spits on LOWELL'S face.)

LOWELL: Let's stay calm. Okay? We're calm now. Okay?
JUSTIN: I'm calm. See? I'm calm.

(JUSTIN pulls rope and a vial from his backpack, opens vial, and forces tablet into LOWELL'S mouth.)

JUSTIN: Swallow that!

(LOWELL spits out tablet. JUSTIN pulls back his arm to hit LOWELL.)

LOWELL: *(Screaming.)* I don't need your rope and tablet!
JUSTIN: Suit yourself.

(JUSTIN puts on his sweater as LOWELL rises to his knees, in pain, and begins to laugh.)

JUSTIN: What the hell's funny?

LOWELL: You don't come close to understanding.

JUSTIN: I understand too much.

LOWELL: You don't. 'Cause I didn't understand. I spent my life trying to find peace. Today, you showed me. Death is fine.

(LOWELL laughs. JUSTIN looks at him with disgust.)

LOWELL: And that's hunky dory.

JUSTIN: You're sick.

LOWELL: Sick? When you kill, when you are a part of killing, every day you are sick. That is happening to you. Your children and your children's children will carry your sickness in their dark hearts.

JUSTIN: Why would I ever have children?

LOWELL: You have a tan line of a wedding ring.

JUSTIN: Fine. I have a wife.

LOWELL: And a child.

JUSTIN: I don't … We're expecting a daughter.

LOWELL: Do you carry your wife's photo in your wallet?

JUSTIN: That's enough.

LOWELL: A photo of your father?

JUSTIN: *(Yelling.)* I carry my father's picture with me every moment, every day!

LOWELL: Let me see.

JUSTIN: Your eyes are too evil to look upon people I love.

LOWELL: Now your eyes become the evil eyes. The eyes your wife, your daughter, your grandchildren will look into … They'll know.

JUSTIN: I don't care if they know.

LOWELL: Caring comes with age.

JUSTIN: Let's go.

LOWELL: Justin is not your real name.

JUSTIN: And your actual name is not Lowell. It's Diego.

LOWELL: Diego. I have not heard my name in years.

JUSTIN: And I live on Long Island. Never set foot in White Plains.

LOWELL: You were wrong about the train. It was the Harlem Line.

JUSTIN: I am not a writer. I watch *Cold Case* religiously. And yes, I read your pathetic novel. It was packed with clues.

LOWELL: You hunted me.

JUSTIN: Like the Mossad hunted Germans in Argentina. Nazi murderers like Eichmann.

LOWELL: I am not like Eichmann!

JUSTIN: Let's go.

LOWELL: I am not!

JUSTIN: Believe what you want.

LOWELL: I am not ... You weren't at Daniela's funeral.

JUSTIN: No.

LOWELL: You never dated her.

JUSTIN: We talked at her bookstore. I took her to a pub, got her to drink margaritas. We compared deep truths about our fathers. Tuesday nights. Six months of Tuesday pub nights.

LOWELL: Is she still alive?

JUSTIN: Waiting for my call. Eager to learn you are dead.

LOWELL: She hates me.

JUSTIN: Together, we planned this.

LOWELL: Lies ... All to find me.

JUSTIN: Two reasons. Confirm you are a murderer of Chilean fathers. If true? Execute you.

LOWELL: And a third reason.

JUSTIN: There is no other reason.

LOWELL: To end your nightmares.

(JUSTIN throws backpack on floor and screams.)

JUSTIN: There is no end to my nightmares!

(LOWELL is frightened and backs up. He slowly checks to assure JUSTIN will not attack him again, and then slowly tries to console JUSTIN, ever so slowly moving closer to him as they talk.)

LOWELL: Sometimes I am forced to turn off the news.

JUSTIN: I don't give a shit.

LOWELL: On my Motorola. A story about Serbia, Kosovo, villages of only women and children. Men, fathers, buried in mass graves. Milosevic denied mass murders. TV news showed children's faces. Children missing their fathers.

JUSTIN: What did you do? Change channels?

LOWELL: I took a quiet walk along the beach. Remembering, trying not to remember, remembering, trying not to remember. Always, remembering wins.

JUSTIN: And you want what? My sympathy?

LOWELL: No sympathy. No forgiving. No forgetting. I just want … you to live as well as you can. My piano teacher, Mr. Amran Bodenstein, survived sixty years after the Holocaust. He died last fall, playing the *Emperor Piano Concerto* for my Albany grade school. A life lived well.

JUSTIN: I live life well.

LOWELL: Good.

JUSTIN: But it hurts every day.

LOWELL: I would guess, sometimes you close your eyes, try to learn from God, learn from some magical place inside you, imagine what were your father's last days, his last moments. What was his name?

JUSTIN: I won't tell you.

LOWELL: No matter.

JUSTIN: Eduardo.

LOWELL: What were Eduardo's last moments? Was he thirsty? Did he have cuts or bruises? Did he think about his unborn son and smile?

JUSTIN: I wasn't unborn. 1982. I was two months old.

LOWELL: I left Chile in '76. Eduardo wasn't in my helicopter.

JUSTIN: If I kill *any* pilot-murderer of Chilean fathers, I am satisfied.

LOWELL: I cannot tell you about Eduardo specifically. I know about other men in the back of the helicopter. Fernando confessed to me.

JUSTIN: The piss and cigar smelly soldier.

(As LOWELL talks, JUSTIN calms and cries softly.)

LOWELL: Men, boys, fathers, sons, brothers, husbands, lovers. Some were well fed, treated like guests up until they were drugged, thinking they would go home soon. Others were beaten, starved, called names, spit on, tortured with stories of how they would die. Some met death after capture. Some met death months later. A few struggled, kicked bruises on Fernando's shins. Some were asleep when they fell to the ocean. Others were wide awake, frozen with fear. Some prayed. Others cursed. Some smiled as if seeing something good beyond. Others looked doomed. One sang a childhood nursery rhyme. Many quoted scriptures. One quoted a John Wayne cowboy movie, in English with a Texas accent. Some gave their Saint Christophers and letters to Fernando for their wives and children. Fernando dropped those into the sea. My nightmares for you.

JUSTIN: It's time to go.

(JUSTIN gathers belongings.)

LOWELL: Wait. My most special bottle of Shiraz. It's had time to air. One glass. No arguing. Calm ... quiet. You and I love our families. You and I desire balance. You and I both kill.

JUSTIN: We both kill.
LOWELL: We drink. Then I go with you.
JUSTIN: You definitely are going with me in my plane.
LOWELL: You will like this bottle.

(LOWELL tries but is too drugged to pour.)

LOWELL: Oh, I am very drugged.
JUSTIN: Not too drugged to talk.

(JUSTIN lifts bottle to pour.)

LOWELL: Wait. Over there. The wide-rimmed, deep glasses. Proper for the best.

(JUSTIN gets two glasses, places them near LOWELL, and starts to pour.)

LOWELL: Read the label.

(Soft guitar music, Joaquin Rodrigo's "Concierto De Aranjuez: II. Adagio.")

JUSTIN: Old people and traditions.
(Reading bottle label.)
"Concha y Toro, Gravas del Maipo. Maipo Valley, Chile. 1996."
LOWELL: Concha y Toro. Dating back one hundred years. And the description.

(JUSTIN sits near LOWELL and reads back of bottle.)

JUSTIN: "Warm, earthy aromas of forest floor and black plum. High intensity of blackberries and bitter chocolate. Full force flavor of smoke and minty oak."
LOWELL: Lovely.

(JUSTIN pours two glasses and lifts glass to drink.)

LOWELL: Wait. Smell it. A hint of the barrel's French oak.

(JUSTIN holds glass at a distance and smells.)

JUSTIN: Possibly.
LOWELL: Breathe in deeper, your head far down in the glass.
JUSTIN: How do I know it is not poisoned? You're suicidal and crazy enough.
LOWELL: Not where my loving neighbors would find me. Now, head deep into the glass. Smell.

(JUSTIN cautiously takes time before smelling.)

JUSTIN: Oak.
LOWELL: Now taste—little taste. The grape. The firm skin and the soft inside. Tannic and sweet nectar. Both at the same time. Mingling but distinct.
JUSTIN: *(Tasting.)* Yes. Two.
LOWELL: Now. No more talk. Only quiet. In the moment. Nothing behind us. Nothing in front. You ... I ... and Shiraz.

(They toast and drink, eyes constantly on one another.)

(Lights slowly fade to red, and then to black as music continues.)

Finale

About the Author

A native of the South, DC Fidler has combined a career in academic psychiatry and cultural psychiatry with a lifetime of playwriting, acting, directing, composing music, and teaching creative writing and the dramatic arts.

He studied theatre, writing, chemistry, medicine, and psychiatry at the University of North Carolina at Chapel Hill, where he served on the faculty. He later served on the faculty at West Virginia University, teaching cultural psychiatry, clinical psychiatry, and acting.

A licensed psychiatrist, DC Fidler has lived and worked with the Alutiiq tribe in Akhiok, Alaska; the Al Moqbali Bedouin tribe near Sohar, Oman; the Kalkadoon Aboriginal Tribe in the outback of Queensland, Australia; and the Te Tau Ihu Maori Tribes on the South Island of New Zealand.

He began his acting career in outdoor dramas, summer stock theatre, and local films and television at age ten. He has written scripts and composed music for over fifty medical educational videos at UNC-CH and WVU. He has written twenty plays that have been produced in various community theatres and universities across North Carolina, Virginia, Ohio, and West Virginia, as well as St. Louis, Sacramento, San Diego, Los Angeles, Boston, Chicago, and New York City.

He consulted and appeared in educational productions for HBO, ABC, and PBS and performed in numerous stage plays including: *Hope is the Thing with Feathers, Night of January 16th, Thieves' Carnival, Blood Wedding, Our Town, A Life in the Theatre,* and *Fool for Love.*

Presently, he is a scriptwriter, film director, and medical consultant for educational films using professional actors to demonstrate mental health issues. In addition, he is an active member of the Dramatists Guild of America and the Charlotte Writers' Club.

Fidler previously chaired the Video Committee for the American Psychiatric Association and served as President of the Association for Academic Psychiatry. In 2003, he was inducted as a Fellow of the Royal College of Physicians of Ireland. He serves on the Arts and Humanities Committee for the Group for the Advancement of Psychiatry where he is co-producing a video series on the History of Psychiatry.

He is author of the textbook, *Psychiatry for Actors: Building a Character Using Psychiatric Principles,* and author of the novel, *Boogieban.*

Plays by DC Fidler
- Voices in the Woods
- Guilt by Association (With RJ Casey)
- Three Diaries
- Sir William Bowlinggreen and Company
- Shiraz
- Anniversary of Miss Nanette Pringle
- School Children Hiding Under Desks
- Grams
- Camp Uni
- Boogieban (Two-Actor Version)
- Boogieban (Seven-Actor Version)
- Ahulaqs
- Elk and Wolf (With Travis Teffner)
- Santee Delta (With Travis Teffner)
- Celtic Crossing
- Stone Touchin'
- Daugherty Park Merry-Go-Round
- La Dynastie
- Gyges Solution
- Begat

Short Plays by DC Fidler
- Persons
- Cruise
- Mobile to Where
- Oman Truce
- Second Amendment
- The Greek God Club
- Four X
- Microscopic Misconceptions
- Drone Guns
- Moon Bugs (With Travis Teffner)

Novels and Textbooks by DC Fidler
- Boogieban
- Psychiatry for Actors: Building a Character Using Psychiatric Principles

Musicals by DC Fidler
- Pied Piper (With Lauren Horacek)
- Healer Man
- Medicine Show

www.ingramcontent.com/pod-product-compliance
Lightning Source LLC
Chambersburg PA
CBHW071125260626

47162CB00006B/2465